# ALL THE FEELS

## Volume 2: A Collection of Six Inspiring Short Stories

B. A. PAUL

# Contents

# Foreword

Life isn't simple and clean. It should be. Right should be right. Wrong should be wrong. But enter the flawed human experience, and our existences rarely take a defined, smooth course. Our perceptions and misconceptions color our opinions. Our pasts and hurts shape our thoughts and guide our actions.

The short stories in *All the Feels: Volume 2* are about that flawed condition. They shine a spotlight on that moment in time when everything changed.

That one decision.

That one conversation.

That slightly skewed perception and the course it sets in motion.

When we see characters struggle with relatable life challenges, their plights punch us in the guts and, at the same time, help us prop up our chins.

To try again.

Give perspective.

Reset.

And they give us all the feels…

Happy reading!

B. A. Paul

# Where the Toadstools Grow

*When Harper receives word of a childhood friend's passing, her grief doesn't behave the way she wants it to. Determined to force the tears, she revisits the girls' shared playground to discover a long-ago fault and a here-and-now forgiveness.*

The decision to revisit Pineville was made last night over a sink full of scalding dishwater with her hands covered in suds and tiny particles of spaghetti dinner. As always with bad news, Harper had gone into one of her cleaning sprees to process, so the steaming water also served to scrub cabinet faces, fridge shelves, and the very back of the oven.

She'd not even planned on doing the dishes last night. She'd planned on letting them sit. To see if one of her live-in adult children would take the mound of plates and casserole dishes as a cue to get busy and pull their weight. Some people dread the empty nest. Harper couldn't seem to get her fledglings to take flight.

But the message had come mid-meal and Harper shooed everyone out of the kitchen. She needed the elbow room and mental space to process the death of her childhood friend. She and Deb had grown distant during middle school then didn't speak after high school, as happens with many BFFs once life and love and pursuits carry people far and away.

Harper hadn't been carried far and away. Her circumstances, and if she were honest with herself, her own choices, had pinned down any ideas of dreamy moves across the country with a load of steel I-beams. So she'd stayed put in her family's home. Sometimes she imagined a black hooded figure with a can of spray paint dancing on top of the smothering I-Beam pile, splattering each long metal giant with their appropriate labels: guilt, obligation, duty, entrapment.

Not Deb though. Her dreams had taken her far.

Well, until now.

Harper had spent the night scouring and scrubbing. She'd disinfected light switches and doorknobs. She'd filled a black trash bag with general clutter from around the house and another two for the donation center. She refrained from running the vacuum because Jeremy was on a conference call with a client, but anything she could think to straighten or scrub without making too much noise, she did. Until his conference call ended and the kids had gone to bed and he forced her to take a breath.

"The dirt will be here tomorrow, Harp."

"That's the problem, though, isn't it?"

He put his hands on her shoulders. Trapping her. Forcing her to face him. "Help me understand. I haven't heard you talk about Deb in ages and—"

She'd shrugged him off and went to the garage where she packed bleach, mason jars, and scouring pads into a white five-gallon bucket. While she was out there, she gutted the SUV of its clutter and polished the interior. By the time she went inside at two a.m., she'd worn herself out. But her eyelids refused to close.

They also refused to shed tears. To give her that release that she needed to sleep. She neither slept nor cried, but she did make an ever-lengthening list of things to clean and purge and donate when the sun rose.

Now, with daylight and the kids at their part-time jobs and Jeremy off to the office, she lugged the five-gallon bucket toward the pine trees lining the back of the property. The trees she and Deb had taken refuge in as children thousands of times. Harper had grown up on this property, just a few doors down from Deb. A standing, revolving door of the longest play date ever, the pre-teen girls had preferred each other's company to anything the 1970s had to offer. Until one little boy came along, that is.

The handle started to dig into Harper's palm, and she switched the load to the opposite hand as she reached the pointed boughs of the droopy tree. Harper sat the bucket down and looked up, the brilliant September rays cutting through the treetops. The longer she stared, the more pinecones she spotted dangling from the tips of the boughs. Some snug in tight clusters. Some alone, swaying gently from a faint breeze that didn't quite reach Harper's lower elevation. A ruckus in a few pines over caught her attention. A young gray squirrel, a little too frisky, had missed his intended branch and clung to the tip of another, bouncing as if on a bungee cord. He regained his footing and scampered toward the trunk out of sight.

Deb would've liked that. The squirrels were one of her favorites.

Harper looked for an opening. It was easier when her body had been a pre-teen and her knees weren't as grumpy. The boughs of the pines swept all the way to the grass, causing much consternation between she and Jeremy over the years. He'd wanted to chop them down. He also wanted to stay married. So the trees stayed.

Harper used the bucket to separate an opening between two trees' wispy branches. A few steps in, and she could stand up straight. Here, in the middle of the pines, a clearing in a near-perfect circle was formed by the space between eight trees. Just damp enough to support a rogue piece of vegetation here and there, but the ground was carpeted with pine needles and pinecone parts. The smell was heavenly. Fresh earth and pine sap.

The girls had used a couple of old quilts when they visited Pineville, the name of their make-believe land. Sometimes the quilts were just quilts, a place to relax and read and journal. Sometimes the quilts held other purposes: National boundaries, oceans, transportation in the form of boats and magic carpets. Harper wished she'd remembered a drop cloth as she sat the bucket down and then sat next to it, the pine needles pricking through her jean leg and the moist earth cooling her skin.

As her eyes adjusted to the dim, she drew her knees up to her chest and tried to remember. Tried to cry. Tried to get that release she was so desperately seeking. The rays cut through the trees in dainty lace patterns, bobbles of light dancing all around her as the trees swayed gently above. As the traffic on the street passed, no one could see her. She knew because for years, she tried to peer into the trees from the road to see if she could tell anything was in here. The branches were too thick. From the outside, this circle didn't exist.

She picked up a pinecone and twirled it in her hand. Deb had loved taking apart each segment and constructing roads, rooftops, and magical wells for fairies and unicorns to drink from all through Pineville. She'd bring her mother's butter knives and scrape dripping sap from the trunks to glue the pieces together. Some of Deb's creations could've won blue ribbons at the State Fair if the girls had cared to join 4H.

But they hadn't cared. Who needed all that when entire universes could be manufactured with a little sap, cones, and needles?

Harper had tried to introduce this magical space to her own children, but they much preferred the antiseptic flashes of screen time and fluffy couches to padded-down, needle-caked earth. And, after the day they'd found the six-foot rat snake slithering his way through the pinecones, the hope of passing the natural playhouse on to her children slithered away with him.

She didn't see any snakes today. The occasional rabbit would hop into the boughs as Harper stood at the sink to do the dishes. Squirrels, of course. Occasionally, a murder of crows would hang for a few days then move on. But no snakes.

Toadstools, though. Harper had forgotten how enamored they'd been with them. The red caps with bumpy white dots on the tops and bright white gills that marched in perfect unison under the caps. How the girls had loved when they'd pop up. And how magical it had been when these fungi made their appearances in their own perfect fairy ring, spores spread and nurtured in just the right timing, right temperature, right moisture to provide a succinct space for their imaginations to take flight.

Several of them dotted the perimeter of the clearing, the light bouncing off their tops. Fly agaric, they're called. Deb had been furious when Harper had checked out a library book on fungus and brought it into the pines one afternoon.

"Don't you want to know what they're called?"

"Doesn't matter what they're called. All that stuff takes the fun out of it. Toadstools make fairy rings. That's all I need to know." And she'd brought out the little fairy figurines and unicorns and Breyer horses with pine needles caked to their sides and ignored Harper's ramblings of fly agaric facts.

Deb was always the dreamer.

Harper stood and reached into the bucket for the glass jars and set them in the clearing. She poured each half-full with bleach and began shuffling her feet through the pine needles and earth. She searched under the boughs that lined the inner part of the clearing. After a few minutes, she started to find the trinkets.

Those fairies and gnomes and little teddy bears from the vending machines. She plopped them into the jars to let them soak.

Long ago, the plastic had given up the vibrant colors to the elements. She just wanted them clean before she packed them up. The unicorn was next. It was larger by far and stuck further near the base of a tree than near the clearing. Harper wondered how many of their toys had been abducted by curious squirrels and raccoons. She was quite surprised she'd found as many as she did.

Nothing was to scale as the toys now are. Deb and Harper had added a bric-a-brac of oddities into their playtime. No worries that the unicorn was three times bigger than the castle or that the little green army men Harper'd stolen from her brother's closet didn't fit the theme.

"The castle is just far away and hard to get to. It's perspective." Harper had said one day after they learned this concept in Mr. Black's art class.

"I didn't think about it. It is what we say it is."

The castle was a gift from Harper's grandmother before she'd passed away. It was about five inches in all directions and held a secret compartment on the base. Harper looked for the castle now, hoping beyond hope that it was still somewhere here under the pines. After searching under poking branches and near the bases of four trees, she finally spotted it sticking up from a pile of dirt and weeds near the base of the furthest trunk. She dislodged it from its resting place and brought it back to the clearing.

She turned the toy over in her hands. The part that had been buried near the trunk kept some of its pink and purple hues, though more pastel now than the vivid colors Harper remembered. She pried opened the bottom compartment, and along with a few pine needles, a tiny square wrapped in brittle plastic toppled to the ground and rested near one of the red-capped toadstools. Harper stared down at the square leaning on the chunky cap of the mushroom.

A note.

And she couldn't remember who'd been the last one in the clearing. Had she left Deb a message after that awful fight? Or had Deb left Harper one?

She picked it up carefully. A vintage communication system

between two best friends. Leave a note for the other. They'd learned to wrap the notes in plastic because the moisture would carry away ink pigments and make the paper hard to unfold. Sometimes they'd sneak out at night and leave a note in the castle if they'd gotten in trouble or if one of their families had decided to take a vacation. Or when Deb's mom had cancer and had to spend days upon days in the hospital, taking Deb away from Pineville for an eternity.

A knot formed in Harper's throat and slid down her esophagus. She toyed with the plastic wrap and it fell away in crisp pieces. She almost hoped the elements had reached the writing. That it would remain forever a mystery. Out of sight, out of mind.

Like Deb had been when she'd moved away over two decades ago.

When the girls hit middle school, the boy stuff started. Pineville was still important, but the friends didn't visit as often. Then the boy. That one that catches both girls' attention and hearts at the same time, even though thirteen is way too young to have a clue.

Harper caught Deb using his name in one of their fairyland creations. On the unicorn, no less. That poor creature, now soaking in bleach, had had dozens of names. None of them stuck. And when the playscape changed, so did his name and his purpose. But on that day, Deb, the dreamer, called him by Harper's crush's name as she planted a little green army guy atop his back and whisked the man off to the castle. Harper, detailed oriented, picked up on it and called her out.

And that's what had started their riff.

By eighth grade, the girls only nodded to each other in the hallways, the boy still dangling between them, and then around sophomore year, Deb was gone. Moved off. Harper'd heard through town gossip and from the fringes of Facebook that she'd taken ill like her mother. But out of sight, out of mind. Harper felt sorry for Deb, but they weren't really friends any longer. And Deb's family, a couple of grown daughters, were perfectly capable of tending to their mother's needs.

One of her daughters had been expecting. Harper'd lost track of time. Maybe Deb got to meet her grandchild. Maybe not.

Harper was disappointed that the thought of the family dynamics didn't bring at least some dampness to her eyes. Disappointed in herself for being so coldhearted and so buried under with life that she never bothered to reach out. Out of sight…

Carefully, Harper unfolded the paper. The writing had stuck. Deb's chunky printing. Ball point blue ink, most likely, not felt-tipped from Deb's art supplies she'd gotten one of those last Christmases.

*It's not worth the fight. You can have the boy. Mom's gonna die. Let's just be friends.*

Harper let the note fall to the ground and she fell to her knees as the note's message punched her in the gut.

Floods of guilt and regret washed over her. Harper'd never returned to the pine clearing after that last tussle. What a little snot. What must Deb have thought of her?

And keep the boy.

Harper did keep the boy. Harper kept Jeremy.

Another load of I-beams fell into her soul. Heavy, labeled with betrayal and abandonment. More guilt.

And all this in the middle of Deb losing her mom to the same disease that would eventually take Deb from her own children years later.

On her knees, pine needles poking through both jean legs and hands sticky from sap, Harper began scrubbing the castle and unicorn and other figures with the scouring pad. No gloves. She felt the sting of the bleach in her nostrils, and though this made her eyes water, she still wasn't crying, just in anguish from the buildup of stress and shame. She tossed everything into the bucket once she was done, stood, and left Pineville for the squirrels and rat snakes to do with as they pleased.

Back in the house, she rinsed the bleach from the figurines, laid them on a towel, and used her hair dryer to blow them dry. She wrapped each in bubble wrap and paper towels and dropped them into a shipping carton. These would be sent to Deb's family. Maybe her new grandchild could learn more about Deb and begin a 'ville of their own imagination.

Harper searched for Deb's daughter's information. From what Harper could gather, the daughter was due any day or had just given birth, but the family was keeping a quiet lid on things while they dealt with the bittersweet passing of one life and the joy of a new one.

As she searched, the little notification bell chimed, indicating someone had sent her a message. She clicked on it.

It was Deb's daughter, Grace.

Greeting Harper. Telling her she'd had a baby daughter two days before her mom passed.

"Mom got to hold her firstborn grandchild. She was lucid enough to enjoy the moment. We let Mom name her. Without hesitation and with a huge grin on her face, Mom named our little girl *Harper*. Thought you should know. Let's stay in touch."

And Harper cried.

---

## Funeral Shoes

---

*After the death of their father, Joey and Shannon have difficulty helping their mother navigate the funeral arrangements. Living in a small town doesn't make it any easier—especially when everyone knows the family's dirty secrets.*

*O*ur family of three gathered around a heavy mahogany table, easily the size of three caskets wide and two long all pushed together. The top is so thick that I'm afraid if I keep running my fingers along the rim's ornate, viney trim that the lid will pop open to reveal where they keep the bodies.

I fixated on one of the floor-to-ceiling windows toward the parking lot across the street. Just a few cars, mostly belonging to us. We all drove separately. I left the windows up in my Honda. The August sun is no doubt baking the dark leather, and I long for the sting of it against my bare legs and shoulders. Anything but the cold of the table on my forearms and rough upholstery of the oversized chairs to go with the oversized table. Mom had rolled her eyes when she saw my cut-offs and tank top. I should've donned my funeral dress for this, as she did. Tell the world we're mourning. The world already knows.

It's known for a long time.

I don't live at home anymore. I like to dress myself.

I shifted in my seat, the chair itching the backs of my legs. The director, Mr. Ulrich, sat at the head of the table closest to my mom, patting her hand and further encouraging the deluge of tears. I remember him lurking at the sign-in stand when my grandparents passed, all several years apart, and I'd thought he looked like Andy Griffith, the sheriff from the black-and-white sitcom that Gramps consumed all day every day.

Tall, built. Thick dark hair. When I was little, I tried to get a glimpse of his gun and badge, but someone always put a strong hand on my shoulder and marched me up to look at a dead body. Then they'd talk about how good that body looked. Or how peaceful. On and on. But dead is dead. And I never once remember thinking it looked good.

Now Mr. Ulrich looked weary. Thinned out in muscle to the point of being lanky, his hair graying and falling—I'm not sure which is happening faster, the graying or the falling. Same deep voice, but his eyes are weary.

That eye thing could be us, though. Our drama tends to bring out the weary in others.

For all I know, his thinning hair could've been us, too. From burying four previous members and the drama that most likely occurred during those funeral preparations.

Across from me, my half-brother, older by ten years but immature by five, slumped down on the table, arms folded for a pillow, head buried. I didn't have to look under the table to know his legs bobbed up and down. Joey was restless. Mom brings that side out of him, but he'd done pretty good helping lately. After Dad got sick, Joey took over the household stuff. Mowing, shopping, upkeep. He dressed in slacks and a polo instead of his ratty T-shirt and jeans. He still lives at home.

But he'd driven separately.

Behind him, between those massive windows, was a fireplace—functional or not, I couldn't tell. Ornate with thick trim and columns framing it as if it were a Grecian work of art. A solid mantel polished to a shine held an antique-looking clock with shiny gold face and stiff Roman numerals. Its hands didn't move nearly fast enough.

Unfortunately, it kept proper time.

Leaning against the edge of the fireplace trim was another funeral home worker. Young. Pretty. Long brown hair and hazel eyes. She looked familiar, but I couldn't place her. Poor thing. Trial by fire with our gang. She took everything in. Occasionally, Mr. Ulrich nodded in her direction for her to take note of something. She'd jot some things onto a clipboard. Once, she left the room and returned with mini bottled waters, privately labeled with Ulrich, Mosely, and Graham Funeral Home. As if families in this room needed the advertising exposure for a funeral service they've already bought.

By the time the family sits at this table, the decision's been made.

Or most of the decisions, anyway.

And she'd brought an extra tissue box because of the mess Mom was making. But mostly the young employee quietly observed our screaming-hot aura. And it bothered me that I couldn't place her.

Mom finished signing the death certificate. There was a to-do about the cause of death. She wouldn't budge the pen until Mr. Ulrich called the coroner—and it's the weekend, so that didn't go over very well, nor very quickly—and confirmed that Dad, indeed, passed from cancer.

We all knew that.

Mom was trying to delay the inevitable. The fallout. The mess.

When Mom's involved in anything, there's always a to-do, fuss, tizzy, or meltdown. Throw her into something like this, even though we all knew it was coming, and she's more than a little high maintenance.

Mr. Ulrich nodded at his helper again as he stood and gathered the finally-signed paperwork in a hurry—so as not to give Mom extra seconds to question any other detail. "Miss Graham, would you please start this questionnaire and obituary with the Powells while I gather the samples."

Miss Graham. As in Ulrich, Mosely and Graham. Maybe I'd seen her here during a viewing or service. Poor thing. I wondered if she'd wanted to join the family business or if she was guilted into it. She moved into Mr. Ulrich's chair. Mom wiped more tears and snot and took a small, shaky sip of water. Joey sat up and rolled his eyes at me. I tried to kick him under the table, but my foot got caught in the strap of my canvas bag and I only managed to brush my flip-flop's toe against his shin. He gave a little grin, then went back to sulk face.

"Mrs. Powell," Miss Graham produced a checklist and sat it in front of my mother. "Here are the options for readying your husband for the showing. All of the local florists, hairdressers—"

"No."

"Uhm." Mom's curt answer threw the young gal. She tried to continue. "We need to know what your wishes are for showing your husband. Or…will this be a closed casket?" The assistant shuffled more paperwork, looking for the missing puzzle piece.

She doesn't realize our family never plays with a full set of puzzle pieces. Or a full deck of cards. Missing a few key colors from the Crayon box, too.

"No. I already went over this. I already went over this. I don't want to do this anymore."

I put my arm around Mom. "We have to get through this part. We haven't done any of this with them. Going through it out loud at home doesn't count, Mom." I tried to be soft and patient. Joey rolled his eyes again and put his head back on the table.

I pulled the checklist in front of me. Typical stuff, so it seemed. "Let's start here. What color do you want the spray on the casket to be?"

"No." She crossed her arms like a stinking teenager. "There won't be any casket spray. I want an open casket. So there won't be room for that big thing."

"Mrs. Powell," the girl started softly, "It is an open casket. But the spray goes—"

"No. You're not hearing me. My Grant wanted an open casket. All. The. Way. Open. Right down to his shoes."

We all stared at her. Mr. Ulrich came into the room holding sample boards and fabric swatches.

"Mom, we never talked about this. If you guys had preplanned his arrangements like we'd asked, this would be easier. Let's keep it simple."

"A casket like that needs to be special ordered, we only have split couches in stock," Miss Graham offered. "I assure you, ma'am, that we can present Mr. Powell in the most respectful—"

"You mean to tell me I'm spending all this money and I can't see my husband—all of him—one last time?" She melted into a puddle, putting her head down on the table. We'd lost two to the mahogany's cold grip.

I stood and rubbed my temples, took a couple of steps back from the table lest I fall victim to its pull. I mouthed an apology to the Sheriff of Mayberry and his dutiful assistant.

"Maybe we put that on hold for a moment and work on the obituary. We have most of the information," Miss Graham rubbed Mom's shoulder sweetly, "but we need a list of family members to put in the art—"

"No. No. No." Mom mumbled into her elbow. "You're gonna ask for names and kin and such. No."

Joey sat up and piped up. His two-day scruff made him look rather intelligent, sophisticated maybe. But then he opened his mouth. "Mom doesn't want the whole county to know what the whole county already knows. Dad, Mr. Perfect. Mr. Grant Powell, had more kids than he could shake a stick at." He pointed at me. "Shannon here's the only legitimate child he sired. Isn't that right, Mom?"

"Hush your mouth, Joe. You've no idea—just hush your mouth." Mom snapped her head up and snapped at him.

"Everyone. Already. Knows." Joey stood and paced. "Got your pen ready, Miss Graham? Let's see, there's a Sam or Sammy in Fulton county—a guy Shannon's age. Over in Marion there's a girl we know about, about my age, Molly or Morgan, and likely a boy we don't know the name of. I know he talked of another daughter born about the same time as—"

"Stop, Joey. Stop."

"Oh, no. I'm just getting started, let's see—"

I intervened. "Knock it off, Joey."

"Well, don't they have a right as much as you or me to know their bio daddy's dead and gone? If Dad would've kept it in his pants, we'd not be in near the mess we're in."

"If your father had kept it in his pants, you'd not be here!" Mom snapped.

Joey's eyes darkened and he stormed out of the room and outside to the concrete steps. I thought I'd see him head for his truck, but he must've stayed in the front of the building.

"Mom, let's get through this."

"I just can't, Shannon. I can't put those people in the paper like that. His personal life on display. And where were all those kids to help when he got sick? None of them came to mow or empty the bedside commode or wipe his drool." She melted into the table again.

I looked at Mr. Ulrich who'd managed to turn three shades of red and gray and back to red again during the outburst. "Isn't there some sort of a phrase you could use, like 'survived by loving family and friends' and leave the details out?"

Wide-eyed, Mr. Ulrich and Miss Graham nodded. She made some notes on the checklist and, while Mom was busy wiping her eyes, she pointed with her pen to the columns for dress and flowers and casket type. Still empty columns. Scary long columns. Like the towering Grecian ones around the fireplace.

When we fill those in, we may set the place ablaze.

I nodded at her and sighed. We'd only begun. "Can we take a break? Maybe come back in a half hour?"

"Yes, Miss Powell, but we have another funeral to prepare this afternoon. And your father's viewing is in a few days. We really need to—"

"I wish people would quit rushing me."

"It's okay Mom. Take a stretch. Walk outside for a minute. Come back in thirty, okay?" She stood and shuffled out the side door toward the parking lot. I watched as she got into her car and sobbed into the steering wheel. I apologized to the director again who assured me ours wasn't the only family to face such strain. How sweet he was as he pulled his hankie out and wiped his brow.

Miss Graham guzzled Joey's unopened water bottle and left for the hallway.

I went to meet Joey on the front steps.

He was smoking. I didn't know he'd started that again. Or maybe I did, and I hadn't processed it. He waved the cigarette at me. "It's this or the bottle."

"Yeah, don't do that."

"I really want a drink."

"Not a good idea. Call your sponsor." I sat next to him on the steps. What a pair we made. He looks like he'd come from a church service and I look like I've crawled out from a rock. I wonder what Dad's other children were doing. Smoking? Drinking? Praising Jesus?

"I don't need a sponsor. I need this to be done."

"I'm trying, Joe. Can't get her to decide anything. But I think I have something that will make the next part go smoother."

"Yeah, what's that?"

I dug in my back pocket and pulled out a crumpled, lined paper with Dad's writing on it. I handed it to Joey. He opened it and read through the page, nodding in approval. "This should work. This should help. At least Dad knew what he'd wanted."

"He wrote that the month before he passed. I didn't bring it up with Mom then, especially after the fit she threw about not prearranging this whole mess."

I read the instructions again. Which suit he liked. Mom had turned in those garments to the funeral home as we arrived. She had a shoebox, too, but I'd deal with that later.

He'd written which handkerchief was to be tucked into his pocket. I'd brought that in my canvas bag. It was the white one with black polka dots, silk. Mom had never liked that. Another reason I was going to wait to show her.

The strangest thing, though, was the shoe request. And now that Mom wanted the casket to reveal everything, that may be a problem. But Dad wanted to be buried in the "most comfortable slippers ever made."

No one knew where he'd gotten them. He'd had several visitors and several well-wishing, chemotherapy care packages delivered to the house. But he loved those shoes. Corduroy fabric in deep hunter green. Black skid-proof soles. Mom complained when he wore them around company, Dad always being the businessman, impeccably dressed down to his shiny black Calvin Klein Oxfords. But the man was dying of cancer, for crying out loud. A few creature comforts could surely be afforded—and forgiven.

I'd packed the shoes down in my bag, as well. I figured the fight with Mom over them could happen here and that maybe she'd be better behaved in front of the funeral home staff than if I'd given her Dad's instructions and argued with her at home.

Given her recent meltdown, the holes in my strategy looked like the polka dots on Dad's tie.

Joey flicked the butt of the cigarette, still smoking and aglow, into the black-eyed Susans growing at the side of the concrete steps. I almost scolded him, but thought better of it. I stood and watched as the ember died out. Too bad, given the drought and the exact right crispy blade of grass, we could've set the place on fire—bodies, paperwork, mahogany table and all—and been done with the ordeal.

But the red glow faded with no ill effects, and my half-brother and I went back inside to face the rest of the arrangements.

Mother exited her car about the same time. Carrying Dad's Calvin Klein oxfords, free of their box.

Showtime.

We gathered back at the table in the oppressive room. Some rooms are that way no matter how much natural light drips through the windows. I'm surprised both Mr. Ulrich and Miss Graham returned to their stations—him at the head of the table, her leaning on the column. Our waters had been replaced with unopened bottles, already sweating. The pile of used tissues by mom's spot were gone.

Mom plopped the dress shoes, spit-shined to a glossy black, onto the table.

Mr. Ulrich took both of my mother's hands in his as he slid the columned paper in front of her. "Mrs. Powell, I called Nesters over in Fulton County. They have a full couch casket, like you requested. As a favor," he squeezed Mom's hands and brought his head down closer to hers, "They're going to deliver it later today."

Mom bawled again. "Thank you, thank you. You don't know what this means."

"Can we do the rest of this now?" I didn't know how much longer I could stand the sandpaper paisley against my legs. I stood and fished out Dad's crumpled handwritten wishes and plopped my canvas bag on the table.

"Here. This will help a little bit." I handed Miss Graham the note.

"What is that? I've not seen that," Mom demanded.

"It's a few things Dad wanted. He gave me that a few weeks before he passed."

"Why didn't you tell me?"

"You didn't want to listen. Not to him. Not to me. Not to Joey." I rubbed her shoulders. I didn't say these things harshly, simply soft and matter of fact.

Miss Graham finished with the note and slid it to my mother. She read it twice. "No. No. No way. Calvin Klein. And now the shoes are important because he'll be seen. All the way seen."

"Mom. This is what he wanted. The house slippers are his wishes." I pulled the well-worn green corduroy slides from my bag along with the polka-dotted handkerchief and gave them to Miss Graham, who took her turn being a chameleon on channel surf—white, gray, red. But I wasn't sure why.

"No way. I'm not signing anything if those items are in that casket with him."

Mr. Ulrich stood and rested his hands on Mom's shoulders. "We've got to get through this, Ellen. For the sake of your kids. For your sake." Mom dropped her head back to the table.

Miss Graham slid into the open seat at the head of the table. She fingered the shoes and the handkerchief and cleared her throat. "Since we have the handwritten note, we should honor that."

"What about my honor? What about what I wanted? What about that?" Joey and I glared at one another. We knew she wasn't talking about funeral shoes. She was talking about the grief he'd put her through with all his philandering.

And she'd stayed faithful. Cleaning up his messes. Covering for him. Doing without so he could pay child support under the table to who-knows-how-many illegitimate children. To an extent, I couldn't blame her for the over-the-top emotional meltdown today.

I looked across the table. Joey'd softened his affect somewhat and was rubbing his scruffy jaw line. In that moment, he looked a lot like Dad. Tall with room for muscles if he cared to work out. Dad looked more like Joey toward the end with the weight loss and scruff.

I was a split. Mom's brown eyes, and slight frame. Dad's dark hair and laid-back demeanor. Along with bone structure, Joey got Dad's eyes. Green in some light, gray in others. The rest of him—the blond hair and high-strung personality must've come from the maternal DNA. Where that maternal DNA came from, only Mom and Dad knew, and I knew better than to ask.

I had asked long ago where Joey "came from." Being so much older than me, I didn't have the common sense to put things together, and some days I still can't keep track. I remember the day I learned not to ask. Joey'd left on his bike for the high school, his last first day. He and Dad had gotten into a fight. Mom had made some comments I didn't understand, about not being blood relation.

When she was brushing my hair, getting me ready for the bus to whisk me off to my first day of second grade. My little mind was whirling after the adult fight. And the pieces started falling in place, but I couldn't see the whole picture. I asked where Joey came from. Why he only looked like Dad. She grabbed my hair in a wad and turned me to face her. She smacked my cheek with the sharp-bristled brush and said it was none of my business. That he was my brother.

And that was that.

I never asked her again. Joey never offered any information.

We don't get all the puzzle pieces in the box. Ever.

He's my brother. That's all I needed to know.

"Mom, let's do what Dad wanted. You get your full open casket. He gets his shoes," Joey pleaded.

"It's a disgrace. I said no." She stood and got in Mr. Ulrich's face. If she'd been holding a hairbrush, I would've had to stop her. "He'll wear the Calvins. Not those…atrocities. I won't be back until the viewing. And my Grant had better be… impeccable." And with that, Ellen Powell stormed out the side door of Ulrich, Mosely and Graham to her parked car.

Mr. Ulrich followed her. Dutiful sheriff that he was.

Miss Graham stayed at the head of the table, staring at the slippers, dress shoes, and hanky. And this poor young professional broke down into tears.

"I think his wishes should be honored." She grabbed a handful of tissues from the box, sending tiny dust particles dancing in the light. "My apologies. I don't know why this hit me so hard."

"Well, I vote for the slippers. Mom votes for the Calvins. What do you say, Shannon?"

"Slippers." I looked out at the parking lot where Mr. Ulrich was bent down near the opened driver-side window. "No. Oxfords."

Joey glared at me.

"Slippers." Then I broke down. "Oxfords. I don't know." I grabbed my own fistful of tissues and the last one sent the now-empty box toppling to the floor.

Miss Graham stood and picked up the box. She tucked the handkerchief inside the house slippers and gathered the paperwork. "How about I make it work. I'll present him in the best light possible with as many wishes granted as I can possibly grant. For Mr. Grant Powell." She brushed a rogue tear on her blazer's shoulder and tried clumsily to shake our hands.

"Thanks. That means a lot. We're a crime to humanity at the moment. It'll be what it is." Joey thanked her again and led me to the front steps. He offered me a cigarette. I thought about it but declined.

"That was brutal," he said.

"That was brutal." I descended the steps and rounded the corner toward the lot. "I think I'll hang here until she pulls out."

"Wise woman, sis." Joey lit another cigarette and took a long drag.

"I wonder what it would be like if his other kids did come to help with this. If they'd get any input."

"More of us? I don't know that the world could handle more of us in the same building."

"They deserve to know, Joe."

He tossed away the butt with the same outcome as before. The building remained strong and tall. Nothing burned except the acid in my stomach and the tears. "We'll figure it out. Have a get-together. Let's let Mom have her way with that, though." We watched as she pulled out of the lot and aimed her car away from the funeral home.

"So you're voting Oxfords?"

"Never. Slippers all the way." Joey put his arm around me and walked me to my car.

～

MR. ULRICH HAD CALLED JOEY. NESTERS' Funeral Home delivered on their promise. My dad would be displayed "full couch." Joey and I'd had many conversations about why it was called a couch when it was more like a bed. Split couch. Full couch. Oxfords. Slippers. Nothing makes sense about death.

Mom had spent the last two days sulking, pacing. And she'd not let Joey or I anywhere near Dad's convalescent supplies. The potty chair, hospital bed, and oxygen tanks all remained right where they were when the coroner had come for his body. Joey chalked it up to stubbornness. I chalked it up to grief.

Probably it was half and half.

At least I didn't live at home any longer. We were hoping that the closure the funeral service would bring would allow her to let some of that go.

Allow her to let a lot of things go.

I tugged on my black sleeveless dress and fiddled with the polyester scarf that dangled from my neck when I stepped out of the car. Not my style, neither the dress nor the scarf, but it had been a gift from Joey. White with black polka dots. I didn't know where he'd gotten it. But it was fitting, given the handkerchief Dad had chosen for his final ensemble. Mom would have something to say about the sleeves—or lack thereof. But it was too hot for a full-body glove.

I waited for Joey and Mom to arrive.

But Joey drove separately. Dressed in the same clothes, washed at least, from the day we'd attempted to make the arrangements. Joey wore slick black Oxfords. A pair of Dad's old work shoes. I cried a little at his give-and-take. Maybe there was hope for him.

We decided not to wait on Mom. As we walked in together, I struggled with my strappy heels in the gravel lot. Flip-flops are more my thing, but I was already pressing my luck with the sleeveless dress.

Joey was venting about the morning he'd had with our mother. "…She doesn't get that we can't wait for eternity. Embalming only lasts so long before—"

"Joey." I ribbed him before he became too gruesome. It was going to be hard enough. The family-only viewing was starting in a few minutes. That would be the three of us. Dad's siblings have all passed. And his other children may not know or have the where-withal to show up. Especially if they knew my mother.

Mr. Ulrich greeted us at the sign-in stand. I took one of those little folded cards with Dad's picture on it and a list of his vital statistics—sans his extracurricular activities—and stuffed it in my purse. I signed the book. I don't know if I was supposed to or not, but Mr. Ulrich smiled at me and I couldn't help but try to check for his badge and gun—for old time's sake.

Miss Graham met us at the edge of the room. I could see the edge of the casket behind her. Too far to tell which shoes she'd decided on.

She smiled at me, her hazel eyes kind and ever so slightly moist, and adjusted my scarf. When she turned to lead us toward the casket, I noticed her hair bow. Not like my scarf, but a match to Dad's handkerchief. White with black polka dots. Silk.

An exact match.

And then I saw her shoes.

Hunter green corduroy house slippers. Not Dad's, but an exact match.

I froze. Joey looked back to see why I'd stopped walking. I couldn't stop gawking at this woman in front of me. She didn't say a word, just smiled.

Then it hit me.

I knew where I knew her from.

She was Dad's. Another one of his offspring. Hazel eyes. The frame. Lean, but room to grow if she wished. Her hair color.

She was mine.

"You—"

She smiled. "I didn't want to upset your mother, so he's wearing the Calvins. I know what kind of man he was. But he provided for me and my mother for years, for as long as he could. We stayed in touch. I'm the one that sent him those slippers. And the handkerchief years ago for a birthday gift." She reached to touch the dainty bow holding back part of her hair. She nodded toward the foot of the casket.

Dad was resting. At least that's what it was supposed to look like. He'd been very sick. Not much one can do with that. But he was, as Miss Graham had promised, displayed in the utmost respect and honor. Even if he may not have deserved it.

At the foot of the casket on a golden wire rack were his slippers. His worn, corduroy slippers tied with a bow, and brimming with dainty sprigs of baby's breath and red bud roses. "When the funeral's over, we'll switch him out of his oxfords and into those."

Joey and I were so taken, we stood there like lugs. Watching this woman, Miss Graham, take charge and honor the father she couldn't have possibly known that well.

Or maybe she knew him better than any one of us did.

She reached back behind the displays of flower arrangements and pulled out a large wicker basket.

Full of hunter green corduroy slippers in all sizes. "In case you want to change into something more comfortable."

I cried. Right into my half-sister's shoulders. And she cried too. We stood there, the three of us. Half siblings.

And mourned my father.

Joey and I kicked off our dress shoes and replaced them with the most comfortable house slippers in the world.

When we turned back, our mother had been watching the whole thing in silence. I don't know if I was more shocked that she'd seen or that she'd been silent.

Joey and I took two steps backward toward the head of the casket. Out of unified self-preservation. Miss Graham didn't know any better and stood to face her head on.

But Mom didn't say anything. She stood between Joey and I and another of Grant Powell's illegitimate children and gazed on her husband. She fiddled with the collar of his suit. With the shirt cuffs around his wrists. She patted his folded hands. She turned to me and adjusted my polyester scarf and kissed my bare shoulder.

Then she turned to Miss Graham and smiled. She went to the basket, kicked off her black heels and tried on a pair of corduroy slippers. She took a few steps back and forth in front of Dad and spoke, "I see why you fancied these." Then she squirmed between Joey and the head of the casket, taking her rightful place as Mrs. Grant Powell.

I gathered our shoes and Miss Graham—my sister—put them out of sight behind the casket. Joey and I stood beside Mom, ready to receive the line of people to give their condolences.

We motioned for our sister to join us. And our family of four gathered at Dad's head wearing the most comfortable slippers in the world.

# Show and Tell

*For Mr. Thompson, the yearly show-and-tell used to be a point of light in the year, but recently it's been a parade of electronics and apps, and he's grown tired. That is until little Oliver brings something out of the ordinary to show to the class, launching the weary teacher into a traumatic reverie...*

*T*he week after spring break in Mr. Thompson's third-grade class was always reserved for show-and-tell and had been for thirty-five years. Two decades ago, the children brought Cabbage Patch dolls and Transformer robots. Occasionally a pet dog or cat would visit the class, with special permission from the office. The class always loved the animals, but the animals didn't always enjoy the visit.

The strangest item so far had been a half-set of dentures from Melissa Spencer's deceased great-grandfather.

Sometime in the last decade, though, Joe had noticed that his students stopped bringing those innocent mementos capable of sparking creative play and imagination and dreams. Instead, electronic devices with intrusive alarms and bells had replaced the teddy bears and trains that blew real smoke from their stacks.

Joe was tired. Not of the students, not of teaching, just tired. Maybe it was all the tech. Maybe too much too fast. Maybe he was longing for simpler times.

This year hit him hard and he couldn't quite put his finger on it. He'd thought of retiring before, but something about this class, these particular students, made Joe realize it may be time to hang up his hat and head for the hills. Or maybe home. He hadn't been back home for quite some time…

Joe stood at the floor-to-ceiling window behind his desk and watched as his teaching assistant gathered his third-graders into a line at the edge of the bus lot. He already saw gadgets and gizmos in most of their hands, and they were already trying to show off their prized possessions to the child next to them in line.

Oliver held a cardboard box covered with a yellow towel. When the assistant tried to peek under the towel, he pulled back and shook his head. Miss Anderson tousled the boy's jet-black hair. Joe smiled.

Oliver liked to keep people in suspense.

Joe tried not to have favorites, but Oliver was special to him. He didn't even know why. Couldn't put his finger on it.

It looked like there was one teddy bear in the bunch. Its pink fluffy head peeked out of little Maria's backpack.

He went to the blackboard and wrote in blue chalk, *Welcome Back, Students. Show-and-Tell Today!* He propped open the classroom door with the landscaping brick he'd painted to look like a copy of *Charlotte's Web* and waited in the hall to greet his class.

He high-fived and fist-bumped and oozed praise over his class as they entered. Several of them were so excited to show Mr. Thompson what they'd brought that they held up the line. He reminded them to wait until it was their turn.

Miss Anderson took attendance while Joe explained the rules.

Wait patiently.

Be polite.

Don't make fun.

One by one, the students showed iPads, gaming devices and music players. Then came Marias's teddy bear, which wasn't a teddy bear at all, it was a Girl Gear Pink Petunia Spy Camera she got for her ninth birthday over spring break. Joe smiled and complimented her as he inwardly cringed for humanity.

Oliver insisted on going last. He watched patiently as his classmates shared, and only occasionally would he lift the corner of the yellow towel and peer into the box.

"Oliver, it's your turn now. Everyone listen respectfully as Oliver shares with us his mystery item." Joe pulled an empty desk to the front of the room so Oliver could place the box up high for everyone to see.

The blue-eyed little boy wrapped his arms around the box. "I didn't have nothin' to bring 'til last night and then dad and me—"

"Dad and I," Joe corrected.

Oliver nodded. "Dad and I. We found him in our front yard out by the ditch."

*Uh-oh.*

Oliver pulled the towel away and dropped it to the floor. He reached in with both hands and pulled out the biggest bullfrog Joe had ever seen. The boy's hands struggled to grasp the unhappy creature, who was using its long hind legs to try to pry Oliver's hands away from its midsection.

The class squealed, some in delight, some in horror, and several girls left their seats, including Maria, who took Pink Petunia with her and fled to the back of the room. Miss Anderson flew to action, calming the students and directing them back to their seats.

Joe froze. Oliver, grinning and proud, tucked the enormous frog under his arm to contain the creature. "Whatcha think, Mr. Thompson? Isn't he just great?"

Joe couldn't speak. He couldn't move. This little black-haired, blue-eyed boy and his giant brown bullfrog had transported him nearly four decades into the past.

Joe leaned against the board, transferring blue chalk to his red polo. Miss Anderson came to his side and whispered, "You okay? Want me to get this?"

"I need some air," he rasped.

"That's fine. I've got this."

He looked down at Oliver, who was still grinning and wrestling the frog, and managed to pat the boy on his back. Without a word, he turned and left the room, closing the door behind him.

Joe floundered down the hall to the teachers' break room, but decided to keep walking to the front of the building when he saw the lounge was bustling with chatty coworkers.

Off to the side of the front parking lot, the picnic tables under the shady oaks were empty. He made his way to the splintered wooden seats and buried his head in his hands.

Joe Thompson had seen frogs since that childhood tragedy, and even a few of them had come to the yearly show-and-tells with prior permission from the office.

But this one... This one.

And that *Oliver* brought it. He'd never noticed it until now.

Oliver, with the coal hair and crystal eyes.

Now. *Now* he could put his finger on it. The year. The tiredness. Oliver.

And Joe allowed himself to remember his childhood home clearly for the first time in thirty-five years.

THE FIVE MIDDLE-SCHOOL boys from Brentwood Street spent the entire summer down at Elmwood Pond. Rain or shine, the boys would meet early in the morning with poles and tackle, tattered towels and swim trunks. They'd walk the winding dirt path that joined the pond with the back of the neighborhood. They'd rough-house, race, or trade sweets from the brown bags their mothers gladly packed for them—a small price the moms paid to gain a day of peace and a chance to clean something thoroughly.

Occasionally, a couple of the guys would break into fencing or sword fights with the rods, lines tangling and fish hooks swinging loose. One time, Joey even caught a rusty hook in his upper shoulder that had to be dug out at the local medical clinic. After the tetanus shot, he was right back at the pond that afternoon.

The days blended into one another with fishing and rock-skipping competitions—no one could ever beat Freddy's record of fifteen skips all the way across the pond, not even Freddy himself. The boys wore out two heavy-duty rope swings before the middle of the summer, pulling them back as far as they could reach on the bank of the pond. The tall oak tree's branch bent slightly under their flying weight until they'd let go over the middle of the water and disappear for a split second before emerging. Multiple competitions and challenges were set, recorded, and lied about regarding the rope swing, too.

Then the Harrisons moved into the once-abandoned home on the corner of Brentwood and Vine. From that home's back yard, the Harrison's fourth-grade boy could watch the gang of adolescents leave in the mornings and drag back to the block just before dark. He watched for a few weeks before he mustered up the courage to ask if he could join in. The other kids his age were all girls. And girls had cooties.

"Well, what's yur name?" Freddy asked one morning when the younger boy stopped the group at the head of the lane. He had his fishing pole, lunch bag, towel and trunks. He already looked like one of them.

"Benny."

"How old are ya, Benny?" Joey asked with extra emphasis on the nervous kid's name.

Benny shuffled his feet. "Ten. Almost 'leven."

"I don't know. Whaddya guys think?" Freddy turned to the group.

"He's double digits. That's somethin'," Mark said.

Doug and Justin circled Benny and looked him up and down. Benny clutched his pole so hard that the red and white bobber on the end shook. "You gonna act like a pansy?" Justin asked.

Benny shook his head.

"You gonna cry like a little girl if you get a boo-boo?" Doug was right in his face.

Benny stood his ground with another head shake, this one more rapid than the first.

"'Cause if you're a crybaby pansy, you can't hang with us."

"I won't. I promise."

Fred stood with his arms crossed and glared at the black-haired mess in front of them.

"Aw, let him come." Joey ribbed Freddy with his elbow. "We're wastin' time."

Benny readjusted his gear and headed down the road with the gang. He didn't say much, but he didn't cause any trouble, either.

He joined in at the pond like he'd been a member of the group from the beginning. Fishing, rope-swinging and rock-skipping.

A couple of weeks later, the six boys lazed on the bank of the pond toward evening, slapping biting mosquitos and swatting buzzing gnats. Mud and fish guts soaked their towels. They smelled of sweat and worms, but no one cared outside of their mothers, who would get together to commiserate about the messes and the odors coming from their beloved sons.

The sounds of bullfrogs and crickets filled the air. "Mom's gonna want me home soon," someone piped up.

"Yeah, me too."

Almost in unison, the boys gathered their gear and swung their towels over their shoulders. A frog jumped into the edge of the pond with a hollow gulp below where the boys stood. Doug kicked around in the dirt, unearthed a small rock and tossed it in after the frog.

Joey did the same, followed by the rest of the gang, save Benny, who stood several feet up the bank, watching.

They dropped their gear and started gathering rocks and stones of varying sizes from the pond's edge. They did agree not to use good skipping rocks, though, which the boys kept in a hollowed-out elm tree twenty feet from the edge of the water.

Justin and Mark went around a quarter of the perimeter, rustling cattails and reeds, causing dozens of frightened frogs to take cover in the warm, murky water. The pre-teens plummeted rock after rock into the pond after the frogs.

"Hey, I think I hit one! That's a point!" Freddy shouted.

The other four tried harder. Benny took another few steps up the side of the bank.

Joey threw three rocks in a row after a frog that left giant ripples in the water. "I got one that time. One to one. The rest of y'all need to catch up."

"Come on, Benny. Whatcha waitin' for?" Mark stomped up to get him, thrusting stones into his hand.

"I… I don't want to." Billy dropped the rocks.

"You goin' pansy on us, Benjamin Harold Harrison?" Mark asked.

Freddy joined in, thrusting another stone into Benny's hand. "Do it, or you're out."

Tears welled up in Benny's blue eyes and he took a few steps closer to the pond. Joey, Justin and Doug watched from a few feet away, but continued the competition, happy to let Freddy and Mark deal with the little girl of the group.

Benny neared the water's edge with the stone Freddy gave him and let it go with a weak plop into the water.

"That's not how you throw stones at frogs, Benny. This is how you throw stones at frogs." Freddy nodded to Mark and, in unison, the boys picked up Benny and hurled him into the pond. They then picked up the rocks Benny had dropped and started hurling them with ferocious force at the scared little boy. Several stones made contact with Benny's head.

Doug joined in. Then Justin. Laughing.

"No, no, no! That's enough" Joey yelled. "He got the point. Stop!"

Benny wailed from the pond, dog-paddling further into the deep, treading water and trying to avoid the stones and rocks meant for the bullfrogs.

But the other four didn't stop.

They found bigger and bigger rocks. Joey tried to stop them and block their throws, but he couldn't go in four directions at once.

Benny shrieked in pain each time a stone made contact with his face.

Until he stopped shrieking and disappeared under the water.

"Stop, I said!" Joey yelled and waded into the water, then swam out to where Benny went under.

The evening light played off the ripples in the water, making it hard to see exactly where Benny may have been. Joey took a deep breath and dunked under, feeling with all arms and legs, making contact with something against his left ankle.

He surfaced for air and ducked again, trying to keep track of where Benny was in the water. He grabbed an arm and pulled Benny to the surface. In the sunset he could see the blood trickling from wounds on his forehead and nose, mingling with the stale pond water.

"Benny! *Benny!*" Joey tried to shake him, but he was struggling to keep his grip as Benny's arm was covered with pond weeds and slime from the water's edge.

Benny's eyes fluttered with the faintest flicker of crystal blue and then closed. The bloody boy slipped out of Joey's grasp, black hair suspended in time under the water.

"Run for help!" Joey shouted before submerging again. The other four boys stood motionless, watching Joey's frantic search. "Now!"

Joey tried again and again for what seemed like an eternity, diving under then surfacing for air. Each time he resurfaced for oxygen, his muscles would cramp and it took him longer to recover for the next dive. He swung his legs and arms out wide each time hoping to make contact. Feeling, searching frantically with blind hands and feet.

Unit Joey felt someone's arm tight around his chest.

"Enough, son. Enough." Joey's dad swam him back to the shallows, where he was barely able to stand after half an hour of rescue attempts.

The residents of Brentwood and Vine had already gathered around the pond, shining flashlights out over the water. The cries from Benny's mom rang across the water.

Joey looked down at his feet in defeat. A dead bullfrog floated by his ankles.

~

JOE STOOD and brushed away the chipped picnic table paint from his pants and the blue chalk from his polo shirt. He brushed away the haunting memory as well, and returned to his classroom.

"You okay?" Miss Anderson had started the math lesson without him. The students had tucked away their electronics, and Maria's spy bear peaked from her bookbag hanging on the back wall. The class busied themselves with the multiplication drill sheets.

The yellow towel covering Oliver's box moved a tiny bit.

Joe took a deep breath. "Yeah, I'm okay. Must've been something I ate."

Miss Anderson nodded and handed the chalk to him.

He approached Oliver's desk and tapped him on the shoulder. Oliver looked up with those wonderful eyes. Joe didn't understand how he could've missed the similarities between Benny and Oliver all these months of third grade.

Joe bent to Oliver's level. "What are you going to do with your magnificent frog, Oliver?"

He pursed his lips and gave a shrug. "Mom says he won't be happy with us. Dad says he must've gotten lost or somethin' and we have to take him down to Mr. Edward's pond right after school."

"Your mom and dad are right. He's too wonderful to live in a box or a tank."

"Yeah." Oliver brightened a bit. "But we did give him a name and took some pictures of us and him last night."

"That was a great idea. I'd love to see those sometime. What did you name him?"

"Benjamin. Benjamin the Bullfrog."

## Penrose Alley

*Diane, a loving wife and mother with a photographic memory, escaped the horrors of the street to start a family of her own. Then the unthinkable happens, and she just can't forget…*

God, please help me not to be a cat. I don't want nine lives. The four I've lived so far have been plenty.

Strange the prayers sent up when your mind has nothing to do. Nothing to occupy the time.

But I know I can't do this metamorphosis five more times and carry with me every memory. Every detail. Every image in technicolor 3-D. I feel a bad spell coming. I'm seeing things.

This morning, I thought I saw David. But MoMo started having a fit and that was a distraction. At least for a few minutes. Then David, or what I thought was him, was gone, and I relaxed.

My back rests against the yuppie diner's brick wall in Penrose Alley. Penrose Alley tucked away from the bustle of the tourists and crowds. The only ones coming and going here are those hauling trash and those considered to be trash.

At least it's warm. I did that part right. Coming south for this regrouping instead of staying put in Chicago. I hate the cold.

I look at the back of Eddie's head lying across my lap. His curly hair needs a cut. We both need a bath, but when your stench matches everyone else's, no one smells anymore.

Trash smells of trash to other garbage.

Or of nothing.

I adjust my weight on my roll, triple-folded to give my coccyx a little more barrier between it and the choppy asphalt. Eddie stirs and continues his midday slumber.

Before the deli's dumpster cuts off my view of the rest of the alley, I can see Melanie and Eric, in a similar position, though Melanie is the one with her head in Eric's lap. Beyond them, Helen's cardboard shack, duct taped and tarped, shakes a little as she stirs. Then the green and rusted dumpster with its flitting flies and bees and dripping grease and soda from the rusted hole in the bottom blocks my view of the other five or so occupants of Penrose. From the end of the alley, I hear MoMo's cough. It's getting worse. The clinic won't see him again. Not after the ruckus he caused there the last time.

I lean my head against the brick wall and close my eyes. I think of David back in Chicago. Of Kallie at Berkeley. I think of the concrete wall across from me with its marred surface and graffiti marks. If a bomb were to take the building down, I could piece it back just the way it is now. I've memorized every gravelly detail of it.

I think of cherry popsicles and thank-yous and broken butterfly wings.

Wings of black and blue with dabs of white. One side perfect. The other side...not. Soaking up the melting cherry popsicle.

And I curse my photographic memory.

I reach into my pack for my composition book and the stub of a pencil, sharpened by rubbing the graphite along the brick or the concrete. Sometimes on the edge of the dumpster. I have a knife which would be better, but I keep that treasure hidden deep in my pack. Only Eddie knows I have that.

I flip through the pages of the book. The one I'd bought for Kallie just before school started two years ago, but never got a chance to give to her.

I don't need to write anything down to remember. I write it down so my mind might release it and I don't have to carry so many weights in my brain.

In my first life, I was a girl. A real, live girl from upper middle class USA. Straight A's and no studying. I could do anything I wanted with the perfectly wired computer sitting between my ears. The girl with the brightest of futures. With the typical doting parents. Well, maybe not so typical. Mom wouldn't listen to me about Dad. Took his side.

So I split with my perfectly functioning photographic memory. Even at fifteen, I thought life would be easier on my own.

It wasn't easier. No amount of book smarts and speed reading can prepare a hormonal teenager for being on her own. And carrying massive trauma to boot.

Eddie sits up, knocking the composition book from my hands. He rubs his eyes and apologizes.

"No worries."

"All good?" he asks.

I nod.

He stands and heads toward our latrine. His metamorphosis had a similar start to mine. He's only eighteen. Two years ago, he told his parents he was gay and they kicked him out with nothing. Two months after that, when I arrived in the city, I found him half starved and shunned, even by the trash. I offered him my gifts first, and now he goes where I go. Tall and lanky, but scrappy as a tom cat. He's warded off more hazards than my knife ever did.

When I gave gifts to Eddie first—food and camping supplies— the other members of Penrose got in line. I shared what I had and was accepted into the safety of their numbers. They're my people. We have respect. Look out for each other. My previous experience —and the loot I carried in with me that first week—gave me a little more confidence and leverage than I had had at Eddie's age.

And when the cherry popsicles and thank-yous start chanting too loudly and the broken butterfly wings flap so hard as to stir hurricanes through the alley, Eddie's the one who pulls me back to reality. Back to Penrose to the unmoving asphalt and stable brick walls and shelter of cardboard and dumpsters. He puts his hands on my face. "Dee. Dee. Mantelo junto."

*Keep it together, Diana.*

Of the dozen or so at Penrose, Eddie's the only one who knows why I'm back on the street. He's the only one who knows why I was on the street to begin with.

He's the only one who knows about that middle life with David and Kallie.

Eddie returns and goes toward the tip of the alley and stretches, but he doesn't linger there. That's the deal we've made with the businesses. We won't cause problems during the peak times. We'll keep our stench in the trench so to speak. And we get free reign of the dumpster when the sun goes down.

He sits next to me and does the daytime stare at the wall across from us. He's taught me quite a bit of Spanish. I help him perfect his English. That and staring at the alley's décor is all we have to do. The nightly feast of half-chewed subs and potato chip crumbs was hours away. And Molly was working tonight, so there'd be no free-bies. Hopefully Dale is on tomorrow—the more sympathetic co-owner who saves back the ends of the meats and slightly wilted produce.

The hollows in our stomachs are like bad neighbors that won't move out of town. I guess that's how the rest of society feels about us. Just move. Be someone else's problem.

I pick up my book and flip through it again. I'd written about David quite a bit.

David tried to save me. And he did; it just didn't stick. A social work student out in the streets of Phoenix for a school project, he wasn't much older than me. He saw something in my twenty-year-old self, and he made it his mission to hunt me down no matter which corner or park or back alley I'd move to. He'd bring food to me. Apples. Bottled water. Snickers. He'd bring me staples as part of his project.

Then he'd bring things to me when he wasn't in school. And when he'd graduated.

I kept moving corners, but he never stopped looking for me. I tried to be invisible. I didn't want the attention. But he was charming. And so freaking determined.

His parents warned him he was walking a dangerous path. Falling for a street girl. Kindness to strangers like me doesn't go unpunished.

But he persisted. Rescued me. Poured in kindness and love.

And I tried not to punish him for it.

We got married and I became that upper middle-class wife that my mother had been—minus the deadbeat husband; David is nothing like my father. I got a nursing degree and a nice job. It wasn't hard. No studying required. And we had a child.

If you didn't know where I'd come from, you wouldn't have known.

I drew a picture of Kallie when she was an infant. Facebook and Instagram had been filled—and I imagine they still are—with memes about "remember these times" and "time goes by so fast" with regards to raising children. I didn't have that problem. Time moved, yes, but I remember everything. From every day.

Cherry popsicles and thank-yous. I wish I could forget.

Anxiety wells in my chest. Eddie sees my leg bobbing and puts his tanned hand on my knee. "Dee."

I breathe and the urge to perseverate passes.

I study the pen-and-pencil drawing of my daughter. She's now the age I was when I got married. She was heading for Berkeley. She's not quite photographic, thank God, but she never studied for her honor roll status.

That day comes back. That last day I saw her, I'd told her I'd be right back with her school supplies. She'd clean the house while I'd shop for spiral-bound notebooks, a composition book for chemistry labs, a backpack, writing utensils. Stock up on toiletries to make the beginning weeks of adjusting to the school year run smoothly. And, as providence would have it, a heavy-duty sleeping bag for her pre-senior year trip with her friends. Camping by Lake Michigan.

All the supplies a girl could need for such a trip turned out to be all the supplies her mother would need to run away from cherry popsicles and thank-yous.

Cherry popsicles and thank-yous.

In a rush, the scene plays out. I feel Eddie's hands on my face, but I can only hear bits of my name and his fluent Spanish. I feel myself slipping, slumping down the brick to the fetal position.

And this time, it's bad. Complete with tactile sensation. Playing out in real-time.

I'm back in my red Lincoln Navigator. The back hatch filled with Kallie's camping and school supplies. And groceries enough for three people for two weeks. My purse sits in the passenger's seat. Pockets filled with gum, pens, phone, my grandfather's Swiss Army knife, and an envelope of cash from the bank. Cash for Kallie's trip and for flea markets with David the next day.

David texts me while I pump gas. He wants to grill out tonight before Kallie leaves on her trip. Can I pick up some barbecue sauce?

Sure. The gas station doesn't have any. This means another stop.

I'm irritated he didn't tell me this before. I never need a grocery list. I don't forget anything. But he's adamant about fixing our daughter's favorite. Determined as always, and I still find him charming.

I stop at the mini mart in the last tiny neighborhood before the burbs tumble into neatly arranged neighborhoods south of Chicago. Not big, but it saves people from venturing further away. Lots of pedestrian traffic from the nearby rent-controlled apartment complex.

I park the Navigator in the tiny lot. An entrance to the north and an exit to the south. All one-way streets around. Some people cut through the mart's lot to avoid the lights. I take my purse and lock the doors, alarm activated.

I walk into the store and the brass bells above the door announce a new customer is on the premises. I walk past coolers of ice cream and popsicle treats. Past coolers of pops and water bottles, sweating in the summer Chicago even behind the closed glass doors. I see an elderly couple checking out. Bread. Milk. Eggs. Lottery tickets.

A mother pulls a distracted toddler through the baby aisle, his little black arms reaching for too-expensive bobbles.

The bell above the door clanks again, and I turn to see a small child. A little girl with auburn locks stuck to her face with sweat and grime. A dirt-stained mint green shirt, black shorts, and pink rubber flip-flops. She stands over the cooler with the ice cream. She's alone.

I go about my business and find the condiment aisle. I pick up two flavors, surprised they have both sweet and heat.

When I return to the front, the mother with the hyper toddler is paying for diapers, bemoaning potty training and all the glories that task brings. I stand behind her until it's my turn at the single cash register. The clerk, older than me by ten years and wearing a crisp, beige apron, rings me up. Her name badge says Faith.

The little girl still stands at the cooler looking intently through the foggy glass.

I pay for my sauce with cash and pull out a single one-dollar bill after Faith hands me my receipt. "I'd like to pay for that little girl's treat. And she can keep the change." Faith smiles and nods and takes the bill. She approaches the girl as I gather my sack and adjust my purse strap on my shoulder. I see the girl choose a red sugared delight from the cooler and follow Faith to the register.

As I exit the building, I hear Faith say, "You should thank that woman. She bought this for you."

I hurry my step. I don't need a thank you. I like to be invisible.

I reach my Lincoln and unlock the door.

"Thank you, lady," the little girl chases after me.

She doesn't see the sedan.

The driver doesn't see her. I have no time to warn her and my voice stays in a paralyzed lump in my throat.

A thud.

The cherry popsicle falls to the ground. A pink flip flop tumbles. Coins, three quarters and a dime, roll and spin to stops.

Another thud and screech of tires on asphalt. I hear nothing after that.

I'm frozen by my vehicle. Faith runs toward the child.

My eyes rest on the cherry treat melting near the tiny, dirty hand. Coins lay scattered. Three quarters and a dime.

A cheap cherry popsicle.

A black and blue butterfly lands in the sugary goo and bobs its wings up and down, taking what doesn't belong to it. The chaos shoos it away.

Toward me.

It lands on the bumper of my Navigator. One wing is perfect. The other one tattered and dull with the tiniest of red from the popsicle. It's at the end of its life.

Then it flits away.

Cherry popsicles and thank-yous.

Then I drive as far south as my gas and my cash will get me. Because I hate the cold. And homeless in Chicago can't happen. David will find me. Kallie will be humiliated.

So I drive.

~

WHEN I COME TO, I'm drenched in sweat and likely water from Eddie dowsing me. That's what I'd told him to do when I reach this level. Throw water on me. He's kneeling by my side with his hands on my face. MoMo and Helen stand over me.

"Dee. Dee. Mantelo junto. Mantelo junto."

I try to sit, and with his help, I'm able to resume my position against the brick wall. I accept water from Helen's bottle. MoMo paces.

"I'm alright guys." They leave.

Eddie stays. "Hay alguien aquí para verte, Dee."

*There's someone here to see me?*

I think my spell must've been alarming enough for someone to call 911. To risk our spot at Penrose. My heart thumps a little harder.

"Who?"

Eddie nods to the tip of the alley. I see an elbow and part of a leg. Someone leaning against the building. "Want me to…" He pounds a fist into his palm.

"No."

He helps me stand and walk to the elbow.

David turns to greet me.

*Determined and charming.*

"I found you. I've been all over Phoenix. I finally found you." He reaches to hug me, but I step away. I can't do another metamorphosis. *Not another life.*

He's telling me about Kallie.

*Maybe I am a cat.*

She's well. Safe and sound at Berkeley.

*A cursed cat.*

"Wait, Diane. What are you doing?"

*Cursed with cherry popsicles and thank-yous.*

I go back to my wall and gather my things. Eddie does the same. Eddie goes where I go. I say goodbye to Helen and MoMo and the others who'd gathered in audience. They understand. They're my people.

"I'll find you again." Desperation in his voice.

I know he will. Eddie and I leave Penrose Alley.

"I won't stop looking. You know how this works." He calls after me. He won't force me. He'll wait me out. Wear me down.

Or at least he'll try.

"She didn't die. That little girl. She's okay. No one blames you."

I stop for half a breath. Eddie stops too. Where I go, he goes.

"I'll find you again."

I know. Because he's determined and charming.

But he doesn't understand the things of Penrose Alley, cherry popsicles, and thank-yous.

---

## Swings and Misses

---

*No one ever gets parenting a child exactly right. But expectant father Alan Wayne knows exactly what kind of a dad he doesn't want to be. It takes a trip to the past and a somber farewell to point him in the right direction.*

here was a time when Alan Wayne had believed in his father. A time when that man stood ten feet tall, and Alan, in his tiny frame and with even tinier abilities, couldn't bestow enough respect or devotion to the one he called Daddy. The one who held his hand crossing the street. The one who showed him proper form for holding the bat. The one who'd taught Alan, at the ripe old age of seven, how to steal candy bars and steaming popcorn from the vendor's stand.

How to cuss an umpire.

How to break in a new glove.

Alan shifted on the bleacher, three rows up and about four spots in, though since the stenciled numbers had long worn off the grooved metal, he could have been sitting in Mr. Turner's spot as opposed to his father's. Close enough for government work, Alan thought. His dad would disagree. Close was never good enough for Mr. Wayne.

Mr. Wayne. A good-hearted swing the man had given at fatherhood—at least early on.

Several swings, perhaps. Many more misses.

Alan was alone in the ballpark. In this neck of the county, people came and went as they pleased. A father/son impromptu practice until the tot tired of retrieving his own misses, and then the sun was in the boy's eyes as it sank lower to the horizon. The balls were packed up and hauled away. They left an hour ago. A mother/daughter power-walking duo, armed with Nike runners and Adidas headbands, the gals walk/ran the crumbling asphalt track that the town had laid around the perimeter to keep the anti-baseball fans happy during the long days of games. The ladies left thirty minutes ago, the pre-teen complaining of sweat and humidity and swiping bugs the last few laps around.

Alan had watched from his spot, well his father's, three rows up and approximately four seats in, as several sets of folks casually enjoyed the lonely field. He kept one tennis shoe on the ball bat, borrowed from the poorly secured equipment shed, and frequently checked the baseball-sized lump in the pocket of his baggy jeans.

He didn't want it to fall out and thud below the bleachers. The ball was, as far as Alan knew, the most fragile thing he possessed. At least for the moment.

He turned his glove over and over in his hand as he'd observed and waited. A Christmas gift. The last of its kind before Alan refused such gifts. He traced the laces that bound the leather into the shape of a mitt. The shape of a hand. He found the lace that, he believed, if memory served correctly, his father had used to teach him a lesson.

When little nine-year-old Alan had grown weary of breaking in the new gift. Of kneading lanolin and all manner of foul-smelling concoctions into the leather. Of pounding the old rubber mallet from Granddad's toolbox and his own little fist until his knuckles were red as beets into the pocket to conform the glove to his hand.

When little nine-year-old Alan had voiced his weariness, and that baseball wasn't his thing anymore, his father further broke in the glove, slamming the back of the Rawlings mitt, thick protruding laces and all, into Alan's cheek. Alan ran his fingers through his beard. The scar was only a silver line the width of a baseball seam, but it had bled profusely down his cheek, chin, neck and onto the collar of his picture-day shirt when first earned. Alan covered it with a thick growth of brown whiskers as soon as age and hormones allowed.

His wife wanted him to shave. Says the scar is barely noticeable. Says the whiskers will prick their newborn when that time comes. And that time was coming much sooner than Alan would like to admit.

The beard wasn't to conceal the scar from himself; he didn't want a clean-shaven face to expose his past to strangers or co-workers. Besides, anyone who knows anything of reality-altering scars knows that the bearers see those thin or thick silvery snakes whether covered by beards, bangs, or blouses.

Scars left by ones once loved scream for attention and remembrance and…

He'd sat for quite some time, watching the people and the sun's trek across the June evening, but it was time to move this along.

Time to get back on the road. Alan stood and stretched, accidentally kicking the borrowed wooden ball bat off the metal footrest and under the bleachers. How many times had he done that as a kid? Sometimes on purpose to play around in the mud and sand underneath. Sometimes so he and his buddies could make fun of—and sometimes poke quite literal fun at—the rear ends of fans and parents and classmates seated above their heads.

As a kid, Alan thought the bats under the bleachers to be fun. As an adult, not so much. He rose and took the few strides to the edge and hopped off. The drop wasn't as long as he remembered, and he jarred his knee slightly on the landing. He ducked his head and squat-walked under the seats to retrieve the bat.

The worst little Alan had to dodge was cigarette butts and already chewed Big League Chew. As he picked up his bat now, he spotted two condoms and a syringe.

He smashed the needle with the head of the bat. He left the condoms. If it had been any other day, he'd been appalled and saddened. But his heart was already at rock bottom with personal grief. There was no room to bemoan the state of the entire county.

Alan made sure the baseball was still in his pocket.

It was.

He sauntered to the first base line and stretched, bat handle tucked between his knees, glove in armpit. How many times had he lined up on this very spot with his teammates to do similar stretching before those monumental games? Halfway between home plate and first base. The field seemed bigger then.

Perhaps it was.

Amanda had wanted to be here with him for this. But he'd refused, and she'd stayed in New York. Eight months pregnant, she was better served, and his nerves more at ease, knowing she was near her doctors.

No, he wanted to be alone. He needed the time and the drive down to North Carolina to think and process. He needed the time to make final arrangements. This was personal. Trying to remember that time when he and his dad had connected. Trying to wash away —and missing miserably—the grit and grime of the past.

Amanda had never met Alan's parents. By design. As soon as Alan had scrimped and saved enough from one odd job after another, he'd earned his GED and ditched the tiny Carolina town for the anonymity a large city brings. Surrounded by people, but unnoticed and unknown.

Where the scars each pedestrian or cab driver or Manhattan attorney carried were hidden under time and attire. And no one passing by knew.

No such luck in small towns. Beard or no, everyone around Alan knew his old man roughed him and his mother up. Mom couldn't or wouldn't leave the one she'd fallen in love with. Why or why not didn't matter anymore. His mother passed shortly after Alan bolted. Maybe, in her own way, she'd swung the motherhood bat long and hard enough to keep Alan alive, then she just…

He shook off the intrusive memory and walked toward second base. The equipment shed—or shanty, as it were—barely held itself upright, casting a shadow over the far bleachers. Soon the shadows would be longer and lower and heavier. He was waiting for that. And to be sure he was alone. The pitiful structure had been all manner of colors over the years. The winning team was allowed a few gallons of paint— supplied by Mr. Wayne's hardware store and pigmented to match the winners' logo-ridden t-shirts. School bus yellow for the attorney's office. Royal blue for the local pizza parlor. Deep purple many times when Alan had brought home the winning run for Wayne's Tools.

A purple as deep as the bruises Mr. Wayne left on his star player if a tourney win wasn't secured.

Alan thought back to the father and son who'd left the field a while ago. He wondered if that dad drug the child to a post-dinner batting practice. Tired and grumpy and longing for a night with siblings and mom in front of the television. Or had the conversation before they loaded up the duffle bag been of the please-daddy-please-can-we-go nature.

The great American sport should be that. Please, can we go? Please?

Not please don't make me. Please.

Swings and misses.

Rounding second and heading to third, the tweak in Alan's knee had begun to work itself out. He'd occasionally whisk the bat through the air, chest level, working the rotator cuff with one arm while clinging to the old glove with the other hand. The ball, snug in his pocket, had started to press just a little too hard on his thigh.

*Don't be sloppy Alan. Greatness isn't achieved with a sloppy work ethic.*

Alan could hear his dad barking at the team. Mostly barking at him. He should be grateful Alan was at least trying to honor the old man's wishes. Giving it a good-hearted effort despite the years of strain and estrangement.

Rounding third. Heading home.

Alan used to know his stats, but he'd since worked to forget them. What good are those numbers now?

Now the only numbers that mattered are how many weeks until the due date. How many days left where he and Amanda are simply Amanda and Alan. Just the two of them.

How many minutes left before he holds his own child in his arms. Just the three of them.

The only numbers that really matter.

Standing on home plate, Alan dropped the mitt into the dirt. He wasn't sure why he'd brought it. He didn't need it. Perhaps force of habit. Ball. Bat. Glove. Perhaps nostalgia—as toxic and sour as it may be.

He leaned on the bat and breathed, taking in the edges of the field to the stands on either side. Home field seats. Visitor seats. An empty concrete pad where the vendors would wheel their concession carts. The paved running track. The shed. He was still alone. He'd been surprised to find the padlock to the shed unlatched—only serving to hold the wooden door closed against the frame, not serving to keep out vandals. Vandals like him, he guessed.

There was a tiny selection of bats, mostly child-sized. A few adult-sized. He'd chosen a wooden one for this task. He'd put it back and secure the door as best he could before he left. Before the sun disappeared below the outfield and the stars and fireflies clocked in for the night shift.

He stood straight and gave the wooden bat a proper swing, standing sideways over the plate. Right hand on top of left choking the neck with white knuckles. Legs apart. Knees bent.

Another swing and near inaudible whoosh through the humid evening.

Another.

When he was a kid the only bats the team used were aluminum, but Alan much preferred the sound of the ball leaving lumber. He'd gone to pro games with his dad enough to know what that satisfying snap sounded like. Snap more than a ping.

It sounded more natural.

More real.

He propped the bat against his thigh and dug out the ball. Spalding. Faded lettering. Official cork ball. Well, not cork any more.

Alan examined the stitching. Red. Waxed thread. One hundred and eight stitches.

Well, probably not one hundred and eight on this one.

Alan had taken such care to clip and unweave the double-strand of thread holding the panels together. He'd done this back in New York after visiting a pawn shop and securing the ball. A buck fifty ball out a of a bucket of dozens. He knew his glove would still be on the top shelf of his old closet, but he wanted the ball to be ready as soon as possible.

After picking up his father's ashes from the funeral home, Alan had spent a considerable amount of time fashioning at least a portion of those ashes into a loose pouch. He stuffed the pouch inside the panels and began lacing the wax thread back through the holes. His hands had fumbled and his had palms sweat as he did this. As he thought about carrying out this wish for a man he wasn't sure he liked, loved, or admired.

Not as little Alan had before the beatings began.

Amanda begged to come. For him not to do this alone. Or at all.

"Let me help. Let me be there." She'd touched his beard, right over the scar. Whether she meant to or not, Alan wasn't sure.

He'd placed his hands on either side of her protruding belly. He felt his little one move inside the woman he adored.

"No. It's my turn to swing the bat. And I want to start my fatherhood off with a swing and a hit. Not a miss." Alan needed to live with himself. A clear conscience to start this new chapter of their lives. Let the past be the past.

Be a better man than his father.

So he sewed the ashes inside. Brought the ball and glove to the park. Waited. Remembered.

And now he stood here. Ball in left hand.

Bat resting on his right shoulder.

He tossed the Spalding into the air a foot above his head and swung, missing. The ball toppled to his feet. His heart sank, thinking maybe there would be where his dad would lay. Trampled on tomorrow right off the bat. All in one spot over home plate.

He scooped up the ball and examined it. Nothing. The laces held. The ashes hadn't slid out.

He tried again. Tossed the ball a little higher. A little further out. Missed again.

He chided himself for not bringing practice balls.

*Not good, Alan. Not good.* His father's voice.

He readied his sideways stance again. He tossed the ball several times into the air, each time catching it in his palm and leaving the bat resting on his shoulder.

One more toss. Grab the bat.

Swing.

Contact.

Authentic. Real. Natural pop of ball against wood.

The ball toppled and spun through the air, not as so many in his past had done, this one had a wobble to it. The laces gave up. And somewhere between the pitcher's mound and five feet into center field, Alan laid his dad to rest amid dirt, gravel, grass, and a busted ball form on the field the pair had spent so much time on.

Love. Celebration. Fights. Devastation.

Swings and misses.

Alan gathered his mitt and returned the bat to the shed, prop-ping it against the wall where he'd found it. He took his mitt and turned it over in his hands, feeling the laces and bumps. Popping his fist into the pocket. He propped it up with the bats and secured the shed door as best he could.

The sun's top rim cast a few last lonely rays over the ball field, highlighting the third row up, four spots in, on the home team's side.

Soon he'd be introduced to his newborn.

Soon he'd try his own hand at being a father.

Swinging. Missing.

And hopefully, when it mattered, Alan perhaps would make natural, authentic contact and knock one out of the park.

# In the Picture

*Crushed by poor life choices, Kimberly simply wants to collect her inheritance and escape the prying eyes of Colton's residents. But her parents' many failed business attempts left no cash—only a dilapidated farmhouse and a stressed-out brother…*
*and two chunky bulldogs who may hold the future among their wrinkles.*

*S*moke from the grill fills Colton's Cottage out on Highway 9, bacon and fried potatoes by the smell of it. The usual smattering of overalled old-timers jawing on about weather, crops, and the deceased occupy the blue-padded chrome stools. All the booths are empty. Midweek, and most Colton residents are sitting in classrooms, tending to phones and registers in various businesses, or driving any number of farm implements. Harvest would come quickly. Busy times in Colton. Busy times.

I slide into the far corner booth. The one that I'd sat in for eons of breakfasts and dinners growing up. Me, Mom, and Dad in this booth. I bet if I cared to, I could get down on hands and knees and look up at the underside of the table to find my engravings. During more than a few of those many grueling family meals, while I smiled and joined in polite, mandated conversation, I'd scratched out "suck this" and other such vents with the pocketknife I'd palmed from Dad's dresser. I'd have been about middle school-aged, maybe a freshman, but not much older. And I longed for my cousin, sitting with Aunt Trudy and Uncle Ike, to join me in our booth. But that was never the case, as Bradley was their prized possession and they clung to him like they clung to life itself.

My brother could join them, though. Justin and Brad, laughing it up, joking. Heck, I'd even taken my brother's company at the table as opposed to being front-and-center with Mrs. and Mr. Arnold. But that wasn't the picture. My place was across from my parents in the corner booth of Colton's Cottage.

Discussing business and numbers and tallies. When you're in the family business, every mealtime is a board meeting.

I'm tempted to run my hands along the underside of the table but thought better of it since I surely wasn't the only wild child in Colton, and others likely stowed gum or other substances previously stored in some body part in the darkness under the booth. And if the eye-level state of the diner was any indication, the undersides of anything could be biohazard. I keep my hands on the tabletop.

A twenty-something, pregnant-bellied girl brings me a plastic-coated menu. I smile at her. She's ready already, pen poised over that tiny square of an order pad, waiting. "I'll need a minute."

She shrugs and retreats to the counter, tending to the old men in overalls and straight-billed hats and work boots dripping mud and manure.

I flip open the menu. I don't think it's changed one bit since I last ate here. A page full of the standard breakfast choices. A half-page of quick-and-easy-to-grill burgers and fries on the other side. They're not serving the "specialty" items on the lower half-page yet. If I want fried chicken or turkey and dressing, I'd have to come back after five p.m.

I spot a combination that sounds good and hope the short order guy in the back makes the order in short order. Some of the old-timers have noticed that I'm here. I don't really recognize any of them, but I don't let my gaze linger.

As my waitress returns, pen poised, I close the menu and flip it to the backside. Maybe I don't want the black-and-white sketch of Main Street Colton that graces the front of the thing staring at me. Reminding me I'm sitting in this ancient place in a town I'd rather forget.

But the backside is worse than the front.

"O, cap M, cap G!" My waitress brings my attention to it. I follow her wide eyes down to the table.

On the back of the menu, there's my family. Our famous portrait. Dad in his straw fedora, trimmed with sage green band, his hand resting on Justin's shoulder. Mom stands behind me, hair pulled up in a paisley blue do-rag, her hand not so much resting on my shoulder as clawing into it.

And there's me. Kimberly Arnold. About a senior. Maybe a little older. Playing along. Counting down the days I could leave Colton and the ridiculousness that small towns bring. And dutifully holding our then-alive-and-drooling but now long-dead bulldog, Chip.

"Oh, Oh!" She bobs up and down, and I'm afraid her unborn child may suffer severe consequences if she doesn't stop. "Can I have the recipe? We *cannot* figure it out!"

It takes me a second to process. I look back down to the caption: *Arnolds' Amazing Cookies: Get 'em Straight Outta the Oven!*

My family's side business. Why we spent so many mealtimes here in the Cottage and not at home around our table. Her and Aunt Trudy in our huge farmhouse kitchen. Baking, cooling, and packaging cookies until the countertops and fridge top and tabletops —and sometimes even the seats of the dining room chairs— brimmed over with steaming cookies. Then the driveway filled with neighbors and gawking-out-of-towners and it would start all over again the next morning. The baking and cooling and packaging.

"Seriously, right? You're Kimberly Arnold, yes?" The Cottage staff and all the old men collectively stares as the waitress beams on. "How'd y'all make 'em? The whole town talks about it."

"Uhm, yeah. I don't have the recipe. I've been out of the picture a while. So, I'll have bacon and—"

"Seriously? You were part of the operation. You have to know your own family's recipe."

I shake my head. "But I do know I've come a long way and that I'm hungry."

"That sucks. I haven't had anything like those cookies since I was a little girl." She rubs her belly. "I'd sure love to share some with this little booger when he's old enough."

She jots down my order. As she slinks back to the kitchen, I see one of the old guys with his flip phone. His gruff voice carries through the whole diner.

"Yup. As I live and breathe. It's Kimberly Arnold." A pause. He's staring at me. "I swear. Nichole just took her order."

Fabulous. I've only been in town fifteen minutes.

I cross my arms over my chest and wait for my breakfast. Unfortunately, Nichole forgot to remove the menu from the edge of the table. The Arnold Family stares at me. Accusing. Judging.

Even I look unhappy with me.

The dog does, too.

Oh, how I wish I had that pocketknife.

❧

I INHALED my country breakfast within mere minutes of the plate sliding across the table. All under multiple watchful eyes of the other diners. I paid my bill and tipped Nichole more out of pity than of duty. I kept my head down, wishing I had one of my father's old fedoras to blind my gaze from the onlookers. A couple of old men wanted to chit chat. Talk about the cookies. And are we finally ready to start baking again. I smiled and said I was in a hurry.

And I was so in a hurry.

With all four windows down on the rental car, a squatty little Honda that's a little short on leg room, I let the gusts shoot through the car and blow the bacon and the encounter at Colton's Cottage out of my hair and from my clothing. I'd forgotten after all those meals here with the family that you continued to smell like the Cottage's offerings for hours afterward. I'd gone nose blind to it, I guess.

I'd also gone nose blind or plumb stupid to how small towns operate. It doesn't take much to make a name for yourself when the population is a whopping two-thousand four hundred. You also can't escape family name connotations for who-knows-how-many generations.

The Frasiers? They're the ones that raise pigs. Always smell like pigs, too. And their son did this and that and got so-and-so jailed because of it three counties over.

The Coopers? They're too good to work in Colton, so they commute. All of them. That's why they've got no money and had so many divorces. Not enough quality time around the dinner table.

The Arnolds? Their daughter fled the family, fled Colton, head full of cockamamie ideas just like her mother. But man, could Mrs. Arnold bake cookies...

That's why I'd left all those years ago. Small town connotations.

But at the thought of the cookies, my mouth waters despite the churning in my stomach from eating too much grease too fast. As my car aims for my childhood home, I note less has changed with the countryside than at the Cottage. Tall corn stalks wave in unison on one side of the road, with the first hints of brown along the edges. Squatty soybeans on the other side. A road in need of repair that makes me glad I don't own this vehicle.

A few more miles to go until the old home greets me. The bright white two-story farmhouse standing tall atop a rolling lawn. Large front porch overlooking the endless gravel driveway. But first I'll see the metal mailbox attached to a wooden fence post. I wonder what color it is today. I'd routinely been sent out with the paint bucket to put a fresh coat on it. White, black, red. One time it was neon green. Then I'd have to affix the weatherproof letters. A. R. N....

That had been the last task I completed for my mom. She'd handed me the paintbrush and bucket. White that time. I completed the job. Stuck on the letters, and, after I cleaned up, I said goodbye. She'd not said much. Neither had Dad or Justin. I'd said my good-byes to Brad and Aunt Trudy and Uncle Ike the night before at the Cottage.

I'd made up my mind.

California was the place for me. I'd answered an advertisement in the back of a crossword puzzle magazine that Grandma had bought after my senior year. Promises of steady work and the opportunity to own your own franchise selling snow cones and funnel cakes on the beach to tourists.

And no winters ever come to California. Or so I'd thought.

And there would be a never-ending line of customers to buy from me while they stroll sunny Cali's beaches. Or so I'd thought.

And a last name wouldn't carry so much shoulder-hunching burden in such a populated area.

Or so I'd thought.

I see the mailbox first, rusted and flaking off layers of paint. Three letters are missing from our last name, indicating Arno gets mail here.

The house doesn't greet me. Instead, it hangs its head, ashamed of the grimy windows and drooping gutters. White paint turned beige in some places, the north-facing walls green with algae growth. Screen door swinging loose in the breeze, the hinges barely doing their job. The grand wicker patio sets, three of them, that dotted the massive porch are gone. The only furnishing is the porch swing, but its bottom is firmly on the wooden plank floor, its chains drooping loosely around the armrests. It's as gray as the rest of the place.

I slow the car down until the popping of the gravel on the metal stops. I kill the engine and stare. What has Justin been doing all this time?

He made it sound like things were fine. Like after Mom and Dad passed that he had a handle on the property. No need for me to come home. Stay in the sunshine. Live my life.

I look at my watch. I'm right on time, but I don't see Justin's pickup. I stand and stretch my legs.

I assumed the property would be in the best condition ever, given the impending sale. I look back toward the edge of the yard, in case I missed it. In case I missed the realtor's sign or an auction house's banner. Something to indicate that Justin was doing what he said he'd do. Something to ease the acid in the knot the bacon had started back at the Cottage.

But I hadn't missed any signs because there weren't any. The money is tied up in the property. In the land. No sale, no money. No money, no plans.

I walk behind the house, where the state of things is no better. The yard needs mowed and re-landscaped. The roof needs repairs, in addition to the gutters. Windows washed. Junk cleared out.

On the back porch, I sift through a leaning pile of plywood signs. Mostly faded-out cookie announcements from back in the day covered in bird droppings and dead leaves and spider nests.

One sign held the likeness of an English bulldog. *Arnolds Amazing AKC Bullies: Get 'em Straight Outta the Oven!*

Wow. Way to recycle the slogan. I wonder if this venture took off. I'd been out of the picture for so long, I had no idea what new plans Mom and Aunt Trudy had concocted.

My plan had been to sell everything I owned. Which I did.

My plan was to pitstop in the middle of the Midwest to pick up my portion of the inheritance. And I'm here now.

My plan was to take that inheritance, book my ticket to New York, find lodging, and start my new life. Head to the opposite coast.

Another opportunity. Another promise of stability and happiness and a name free of connotations.

That was my plan.

Tires rolling over gravel signal someone's arrival. I leave the signs, step further into the back yard, and look up at the house. I hear a vehicle door slam. Then another.

Two waddling English bulldogs run shoulder-to-shoulder to greet me from around the corner. My brother comes from the other side, his head as droopy and as ashamed as the house's.

I bend to the dogs, and they cover my hand in slimy kisses before running back to Justin. I think those wrinkled creatures may be the embodiment of my inheritance.

The knot in my stomach gives birth to more knots.

My plan was so solid.

Or so I'd thought.

I HAVEN'T WALKED through the house yet. After the shock of the exterior and the stark emptiness of the living room, I'd frozen in place. So we sit in the living room on a tripled-up blanket and lean against the wall facing the fireplace. As if we're waiting for gathering family to celebrate something. Waiting for the fire to pop to life as Dad stoops over, tips his fedora back on his head so it won't fall into the embers, and coaxes the sparks and logs to do their job.

But this is no celebration. Justin had sold everything he could to satisfy the creditors and buy more time to think. More time for me to arrive to put my worthless two cents' worth in. And that's what I'm feeling now. Worthless.

The dogs snort and explore the downstairs level as if they'd not been in the house before. I wonder if their stubby legs could scale the steps. "They're worth a few hundred, right?" I nod to the dogs.

"They'd have been worth a few thousand if Mom and Dad could've parted with them as pups. Now they're old and stink. Not everyone finds the adult versions so charming." One of them comes and lays longways next to Justin's legs, drooping drooling jowls over his shin. "I can't do it. Relocate them. Can we, Meg? Can we, Meg?" He reaches down and smacks the dog on her rear. She looks back at him and her tongue rolls out of her mouth, dragging a trail of slobber with it.

"Good grief, Justin." The other dog, the male, joins me on my side of the blanket. He's a wrinkled bowling ball with legs. He lies down, head facing me, thank goodness, because I think he's got some stomach issues. Justin's gone nose blind to them by now, no doubt. Our old Chip used to smell like a compost pile most of the time. Sweet dogs, though.

"That one's Tartar. Meg and Tartar."

"Like stuff you dip fish in? That's fitting. He smells like it."

"No. Cream of Tartar. Must be the coloring or something. Mom named him before…"

Before she died and I didn't have the funds nor the mental functioning to come home for the service. They didn't have the money to bury her, either, so Justin and I agreed to do something with her ashes once I came back this way. Dad's were scattered at the edge of Colton at the fishing pond. Mom hated that fishing pond, but maybe that's where she'd have to go…

I take a deep breath and try to relax my shoulders against the wall. I try to think. But that deep breath brought the in ever-so-faint aroma of cookies. It hangs in the air. The entire house used to smell of brown sugar and melting chocolate. It still lingers above the dust and dog and sad emptiness.

"At some point, we'll have to go over the paperwork. We're upside down. Even auctioning the property won't solve much. Then I'm left with nowhere to live because I sank all my cash into trying to bail them out of their last enterprise." He puts "enterprise" in air quotes.

"Why didn't you tell me, Just?"

He shrugs. "You'd escaped. I didn't want to bother my kid sister with stuff I should be able to handle."

"I didn't escape." I draw my knees up to my chest. "Maybe I escaped the town and the atmosphere here, but I'm my mother's child. Grand ideas, poor execution."

"So no sources to tap for funds to get us out from under this?"

"When I pulled in the drive, I had a plan and two bags of clothes in the trunk. Now I have two bags of clothes in the trunk." I study my brother's face. Crow's feet and worry lines and smattering of gray. I see my features in his facial structure. Square jaw, thin lips. Old and stressed.

"How pathetic. How did relatively intelligent middle-aged humans get done in by Arnolds' cookies and bulldogs?" Justin shakes his head, and Meg, with perfect timing, lets one rip that lasts two seconds. We can't help but laugh. Then we had to stand to get away from the fumes.

"Well, let's see the rest of it. Grand tour, Brother?"

He gives me his arm, like we're going on a date, and leads me up the staircase off the side of the living room. To my surprise, the dogs pop up and lead the way, their butts and curly stubbed tails struggling on the wooden planks.

The family photos of fedoras and bulldogs and cookie-baking still line the stairs. I run my hand against the bumpy plaster and tug on the wooden frames. The last few eight-by-tens only have three humans. Several dogs. No Kimberly. I wasn't in the picture for those.

Mom and Dad's room is as barren as the living room. One Rubbermaid tote sits next to the wall. I pop the lid off and will myself not to fall to my knees. "I just couldn't get rid of those. Maybe a few hundred bucks' worth, but that's what I kept of Dad's. Take what you want," Justin says.

Dad's fedoras. Dumb hats. Having them all in one place and closed up, when the lid came off, I could smell *him*. Over the dogs. Over the brown sugar. His aftershave mingled with sweat. Faint but lingering. Straw, felt, wide and short-brimmed. I could see him grinning from under them all.

I try to focus on something else. "Speak to Bradley?"

"Got two kids. He and his wife aren't much better off. Trudy and Ike, well…"

I nod. Somehow, the four most prominent adults in our lives all had the get-rich-quick and pie-in-the-sky genes. Ventures and investments and businesses. And it all went down in those booths in the back of Colton's Cottage.

"Needless to say, Bradley's become a commuter now. Spends most of his time at a job he hates—or driving to it."

I peek into Justin's room. A double bed, unmade. Boxes of clothes. No dresser. No nightstand. A black radio with extended silver antennae is plugged into the wall and sits on the floor. Meg and Tartar scale the bed and take nest, one near the head, the other near the foot.

"You live like a hobo."

"I have about as much money as one, too."

"Likewise."

We continue to my bedroom. I open the door. The hinges still grunt with the effort. "I saved personal stuff. Everything else, well..." Justin shuffles his feet and hung his head. I hate seeing my brother this way. He and Bradley had been so carefree. So full of orneriness and vigor. Now...

I put my arm around him and squeeze hard. "I know. It's okay. We'll figure something out."

"I've thought about Mexico."

"Canada's closer."

We stand in the hallway and peer into my bedroom. Three cardboard boxes with "Kimberly" scrolled across the tops were the only three things in the room. Even the curtains were gone.

"You can take my bed. I'll sleep on the floor with the mutts."

I look across the hall to his bed. The dogs raise their heads and look back. "I don't think so."

We go downstairs to the kitchen. The dogs preferred to stay upstairs for their mid-morning comas.

The cookie essence is strongest in this room. The massive farmhouse table is gone. The fridge stayed. I pop it open. Sodas and a gallon of milk. I pull out the lunch meat, looking for an expiration date.

"I wouldn't trust it."

Justin tells me of his job helping Mr. Frasier with the farm and the swine. Their family is as much of a mess as ours. In return for a meager wage, Mrs. Frasier pumps Justin—and the Bullys—full of home-cooked goodness. For which he is truly grateful. He's not home much, it looks like.

I pop open one of the cabinets. Shiny, stainless steel colanders and mixing bowl sets nearly topple out. "Justin! These were high end. Why do you still have them?"

"I put them in the personal property auction. No one would bid."

"You've got to be kidding me. All the farm wives and even the Cottage would've wanted Mom's cooking gear." I pull out more and more pieces. Mixers, food processors. Another cabinet had measuring cups, cooling racks, spatulas, and industrial-sized mixing bowls. I empty the cabinets onto the countertop and floor to take stock.

"The locals refused to bid. Ticked off the auctioneer. They said we'd need it again. They said we could figure out the recipe and start over."

I open a long drawer next to the sink. Mom's well-loved aprons lay neatly folded and stacked. "Those I didn't offer. I kept those on purpose. Didn't even unfold them."

I take two from the drawer, the green one with little strawberries all over and the cream one with Cookie Monster embroidered on the pockets. Two wooden stools missing most of their red paint are nudged against the cabinets and I take the one nearest me. I stretch out the strawberry apron and shake it hard, then slide the strap around my neck and tie the waist. The pockets along the front are stained and fraying at the edges, so I try not to toy with them. "Okay. So we have mementos no one cares about. Aprons. Fedoras. Cooking gear. Two dogs and a shell of a house."

"And don't forget the expired lunch meat." Justin leans against the fridge.

I smooth open the Cookie Monster apron and slide off the stool. I drape the strap around Justin's neck and spin him away from the fridge so I can tie the strings in the back. He pats the pockets.

"What's this?"

He pulls out a folded piece of lined notebook paper and hands it to me.

I take it from him and flick it open. "Does anyone ever ask you about the cookies? The recipe?"

"Yeah. Not a day or two goes by someone doesn't ask me. Beg me sometimes, especially around the holidays or someone's birthday."

"Ever find it? The recipe?"

"Found lots of them. Not *the recipe*, though."

We examine the paper as I uncrease it. Mom's handwriting. The title at the top of the short-hand, coded recipe says: *THIS IS THE ONE.*

Justin's eyes widen and he snatches it from me.

"Careful. It's fragile."

"I don't know what this stuff means. Do you?"

"No. But get that bowl." Justin reaches for the small one on the counter. "No. The big one. I've got an idea."

I bound up the stairs to retrieve two more pieces of the puzzle before meeting Justin in the drive where I plop one of Dad's fedoras onto his head, and another onto mine.

"Where are we going?" Justin helps me pack the industrial mixing bowl, two farting dogs and, donning aprons and fedoras, I instruct him to point the pickup toward the Cottage.

"Suddenly I'm in the mood for fried chicken."

I TIE Meg to the grocery store's bike rack while Justin ties Tartar. The dogs had fared well with similar treatment at Colton's Cottage while Justin and I ate dinner. Everyone knew Meg and Tartar. They were Arnolds, after all. And, according to my brother, regulars down at the Cottage.

The drive to the supermarket one county over had been punctuated with moments of silent contemplation and other stretches of intense processing of the "I can't believe they went for it" variety while the dogs snored in the back seat. The industrial-sized mixing bowl clanged on the floorboard, overflowing with bills in every denomination. Mostly five's, but all presidents represented well.

Nichole had taken an extra shift, my waitress for the second time today, and served Justin and I more than our fair share of fried chicken. She'd even made a sign for the bowl, which she displayed proudly on the counter, front and center: *Help Arnolds' Cookies Come Back in the Picture.* The sign also explained, so we wouldn't have to repeat ourselves quite so much, that we'd be giving away our first attempt—so don't get your hopes up—in two weeks at the Cottage as a way to say thanks for helping.

Before tying up the dogs, we lost the hats and aprons and stuffed our pockets with the cash so as not to look like our parents. Too much.

"Which aisle?"

I skim the signs hanging overhead for baking supplies. Justin grabs a cart while I fish out Mom's scribbled recipe.

We find the aisle and get to work. We could assume some of the shorthand was straightforward. Fl for flour. CC for chocolate chips. BS for brown sugar and not the alternative, though we did have a good attention-drawing laugh discussing how maybe BS really was the secret ingredient. MDU v WN after much consternation we agree must be macadamia nuts versus walnuts, so we get both. And we can afford it for this first trial run, which I'm still in shock over.

This morning, the Colton locals were rude and pushy and a little too in-your-business. Or so I'd thought.

This evening, after the outpouring of support, endearing is the only way I could describe them.

Now, two ingredients left, NM and COT. We scan the spices twice and venture two aisles in either direction on the chance we are way off base.

"Don't you remember?" Justin's impatience mounts. He'd been to the front of the store twice to check on the dogs. One time he came back with an extra twenty bucks when he'd ran into another Colton family shopping here.

"I never helped measure stuff out. They did that, Mom and

Trudy. I only stirred and cooled and packaged and painted the mailbox."

"Tartar's getting grumpy. It's past his bedtime."

"It's probably always past that dog's—" I stop myself and grab my brother by his weary shoulders. "What's that dog's name again?"

"Tartar."

"No. The whole thing."

"Cream of—" Justin face palms himself.

"COT," we say in unison. We found the tiny container. The measurements listed for a giant batch were also tiny.

"Some of these things are expensive. I hope she knew what she was doing."

"One more. NM."

"Does the female have a middle name?" I joke as I begin scanning the spices once more.

"No." This time Justin grabs my shoulders, laughing. "Her name's *Nutmeg*."

∼

THREE MONTHS after my arrival to Colton, and I'm a true Arnold again. Baking. Stirring. Cooling. Packaging. The freebie thank-you batches down at the Cottage were a success and brought in even more donations. I have a mattress with sheets and everything. And there's a couch in the living room. Mr. Frasier even built us an oversized farmhouse table. We declined a television, preferring to listen to Justin's old radio over the screen. Who has time for TV?

Busy times in Colton. Busy times.

After we'd hit the right balance with tastes and textures, Justin and I brought in Bradley's wife to help. Bradley's even thinking of cutting back hours on his commute job to do some special deliveries, but we're trying to be smarter this time. Take it slow. Don't add too much too fast and get in the same mess our parents had.

We will be adding Nichole part time once she's up to it, though. She's been a key instrument with her enthusiasm and bubbly personality. Bubbly is something the Arnolds lack. And I promised myself I wouldn't make her do ridiculous tasks like paint the mail-box. Unless she wanted to, that is.

I finish cleaning up the day's baking and secure the front door, latching a brand-new screen. Nutmeg and Tartar snore on the couch. They've yet to adjust to their new fast-paced cookie-baking lifestyle. "Up to bed, you two, or we'll sell you to the first customers in the morning." They stretch and tumble off the sofa. I follow the four-legged butterballs up the steps and run my fingers across the frames of the Arnold family history that guards the staircase.

I pause at the most current frame. Justin, Bradley and his wife. Their two kids. Nichole, who'd protested, but we forced her. Nutmeg and Cream of Tartar, smiling and slobbering as they look up at the humans. And me.

Contented peace settles deep in my stomach. The knot is still there sometimes—probably too many board meetings at the Cottage. But mostly, it's peace.

I'm in the picture.

# About the Author

Beth enjoys chucking words into sentences then standing back to see what magic—or mayhem—falls out, crafting tales in mystery, sci-fi, fantasy, and general "slice of life" fiction. She couldn't accomplish this without the help of her tutu-clad Little Miss Muse and Trudi the Concrete Office Goose, who's partial to superhero capes.

Her stories have appeared in multiple publications, including Pulphouse Fiction Magazine and Ellery Queen Mystery Magazine, and in multiple fiction anthologies. She's received several Honorable Mentions from Writers of the Future. Her lighthearted blog peeks into the writing life as she pokes fun at herself and her circus of a life.

Follow the antics of Little Miss Muse and Trudi, read Beth's blog (she might have burned down her kitchen last week), and discover the stories at bapaul.com.

# Also by B. A. Paul

**Short Story Collections**

Spunk and Spice, Volumes 1 and 2: A Collection of six short stories celebrating timeless wit and wisdom.

Out There, Volumes 1 and 2: A Collection of six short sci-fi and speculative tales.

Mystery Minutes, Volumes 1 and 2: Six short mystery stories

All the Feels, Volumes 1, 2, and 3: Collections of inspiring short stories

Just a Tick of Whimsy, Volumes 1 and 2: Collections of fantasy shorts.

Hijacked Holidays: Definitely not your warm-and-fuzzy winter tales.

Dark Minds: Toe-curling twisted mysteries.

**Blog Compilations: Slices of the writing life with lots of laughs and bumps in the road.**

Life Along the Way

Life All Over Again

**Novels**

Triage

**Young Adult (or Young at Heart) Books**

Switch: Book 1 in the Oliver Andrews Trilogy

---

## Stay In Touch!

---

### BAPAUL.COM

Take a glimpse into B.A. Paul's writing journey, including the ups and downs of managing family, "real jobs," ducks in wobbling rows, and chasing down her Little Miss Muse. New blog posts go up Mondays, with the first Monday of the month reserved for a free fiction short story available on the blog for a limited time.

Newsletter Signup!

Get the latest release information, author updates, and exclusive content by signing up at bapaul.com.